Translated from the French *Comment rallumer un dragon éteint*

First published in the United Kingdom in 2019 by
Thames & Hudson Ltd, 181A High Holborn,
London WC1V 7QX

www.thamesandhudson.com

First published in the United States of America in 2019 by
Thames & Hudson Inc., 500 Fifth Avenue, New York, New York 10110

www.thamesandhudsonusa.com

Original edition © 2016 Éditions Sarbacane, Paris
English translation rights arranged through La Petite Agence, Paris
This edition © 2019 Thames & Hudson Ltd, London

British Library Cataloguing-in-Publication Data
A catalogue record for this book is available from the British Library

Library of Congress Control Number 2018962327

ISBN 978-0-500-65197-1

Printed and bound in Malaysia

Didier Lévy   Fred Benaglia

HOW TO LIGHT your dragon

Thames & Hudson

Has your pet dragon's fire
GONE OUT?

....

don't worry.
THERE MUST BE A WAY
TO RELIGHT HIM!

PERHAPS SOMETHING'S BLOCKING HIS FLAMES

HIS FLAMES

Try lifting up his back legs AND GIVING HIM A GOOD SHAKE

MAYBE HE NEEDS A NEW SPARK!

A GOOD WAY TO MAKE A SPARK IS TO FIND A FEATHER DUSTER

AND TICKLE YOUR DRAGON

TICKLE HIS FEET ...

UNDER
HIS ARMS
...

AND THE TIP OF HIS NOSE

STILL NOTHING?

NO EXPLOSIONS?

TAKE YOUR DRAGON SHOPPING.
THEN SHOW HIM THE LATEST OVENS
AND SING THEIR PRAISES.

HOW ABOUT THIS— MAKE FAKE FLAMES OUT OF **RED** AND **YELLOW** PAPER, AND STICK THEM TO THE END OF HIS NOSE!

(Better than nothing, RIGHT?)

BUT WHAT IF YOUR DRAGON SWALLOWS THE PAPER FLAMES, FLOPS DOWN AND REFUSES TO MOVE? WELL, THEN YOU'VE GOT A **REAL PROBLEM.**

AND ALL THE ADVENTURES YOU'VE HAD TOGETHER.